A Werewolf in Mims

Also by J. Lynn Carr

Griffinwood Close
Wish You Were Here

A Werewolf in Mims

J. Lynn Carr

pagethirteen

Wild Roots paperback edition May 2024

Book design by J. Lynn Carr

ISBN: 979-8-9882084-5-7 (Wild Roots edition paperback)

www.pagethirteenpress.com

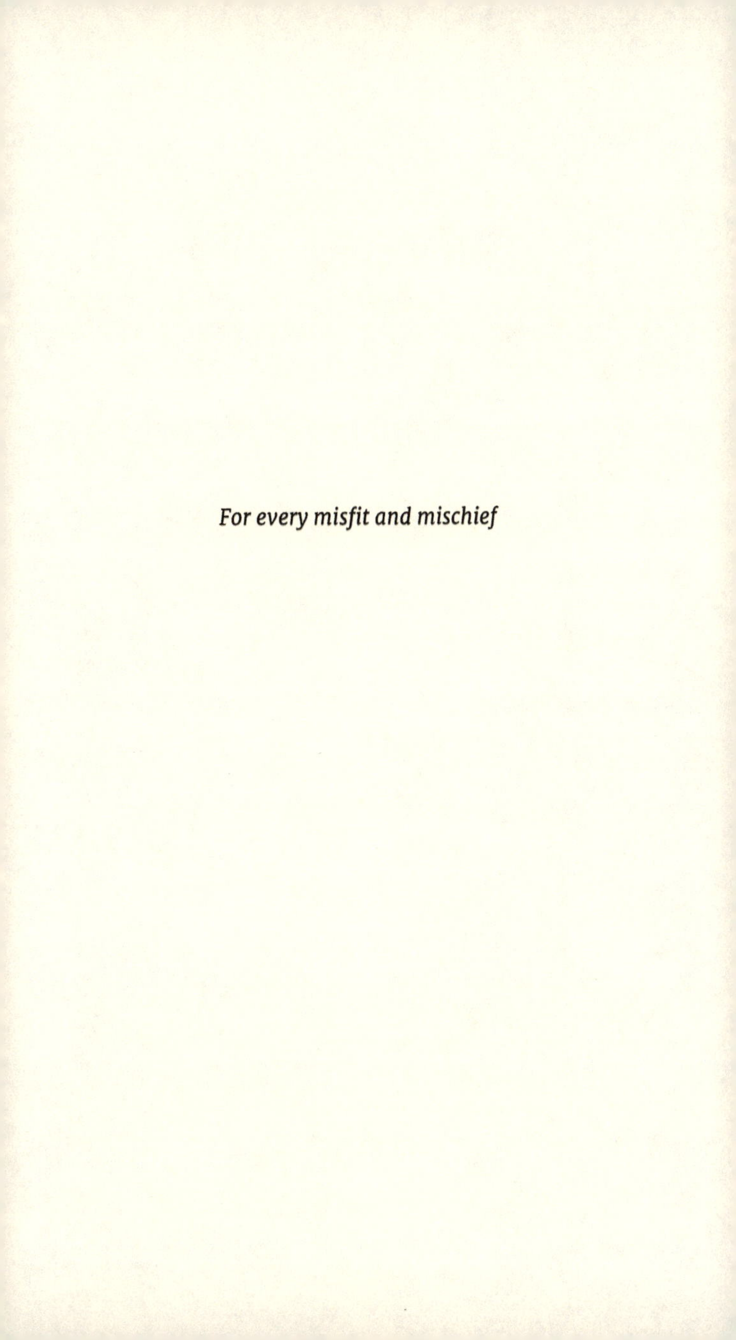

For every misfit and mischief

Author's Note

A Werewolf in Mims is one of the first stories I self-published, and I was (still am) immensely proud of it.

This republished edition does not tamper with the story too much, though some parts have been edited for clarity and consistency. The most notable changes are visual, with a smaller trim size and custom design elements.

However, since this story has now gone through even more rounds of editing and proofreading, I have no excuses for any remaining typos, except, perhaps, for the fact that I am human.

Thank you for joining me in this little pocket of the universe that I've created.

Happy reading,
J. Lynn Carr

Part I

The Howl Heard Across Mims

Chapter 1

Everyone in Mims suspected that the newcomer was a werewolf but it wasn't until the first full moon after Hamish Kelly was bitten that they knew for sure.

Although by no means geographically isolated, Mims is still made up of space—sprawling emerald fields populated more by cows and sheep than people. There is a small town square with a grocery store, a church, a library, and a pub—but Hamish's home is on the outskirts, the last address before the town line. Indeed, he is the farthest he can be from the town square and still call Mims his home.

This is perhaps why it took everyone a bit longer to catch onto to his predicament.

Hamish breathes in the morning air,

tinged with the smell of freshly brewed coffee and ice. His hand is wrapped haphazardly, but effectively. The wound itself bled for three days but has just begun to heal, skin stitching itself together with a preternatural speed. The tug of the moon beats a constant song in his heart, a reminder that he will need to make some adjustments to his home and his lifestyle.

He turns to look at the fields that make up the bulk of his property. Once, they held rows and rows of trees—oranges, grapefruit, and peaches bursting from the branches. Behind that, were vibrant rows of lettuce and tomatoes, and a few bunches of strawberries so sweet that everyone in Mims swore the Kellys must be witches. In the back, there was a wild grapevine that he would tame just enough to make a few bottles of wine to keep at the back of the pantry every summer.

But now the fields are bare, peppered only by a few sheep that must have broken out of the Appleton farm next door. He can see the Appleton house in the distance, a tall, white rectangle with a wraparound porch and a detached red barn just to the left of it.

He's not sure how the transformation will

work and he wishes his neighbors—Frank and Mary Appleton, and their son, Billy—were out of town, or a little farther away at least. He shudders to think that he might hurt one of them.

Or *anyone* for that matter.

Perhaps he will retain some sort of consciousness or a presence of mind? He certainly hopes so.

Not for the first time, he thinks he should tell someone about his current predicament. Surely, they will have noticed the wound on his hand, his bandage soaked with blood no matter how tightly he wrapped it. It was quite obvious, and he made no attempt to hide it the last time he went down to the pub. Worse though, is the fear that everyone already knows about his upcoming transformation but feels that it's not their problem.

More like, people are busy these days, he thinks. And anyway, he can take care of himself, even now that Emmeline is no longer with him.

He takes a moment to think of his wife. The remnants of her favorite plant, a wisteria vine she planted in their first year of marriage, are still clinging to the side of the house and although it hasn't bloomed since she passed, he swears he can smell the purple flower on the edges of the wind.

———◆———

Soon, he begins to feel the fire in his veins grow hotter. The tang of copper sits permanently under his tongue now, a thirst that cannot be quenched by water. His vision becomes cloudy with red. The sudden desire to run barefoot across the field seizes him almost completely.

He could give in, but there is still work to do. He manages to find a steel chain and padlock for the door, hidden among the remnants of a life he can no longer live. He orders a few extra pounds of raw meat with Tim, the butcher, to help him through the next week or so. He trades a few of the nicer steaks with the Appletons, in exchange for the leftover timber from their recent barn renovation.

He uses it to board up his windows, working on the assumption that the beast growing inside of him will emerge on the full moon hungry and thirsty for a meal he would quickly regret.

Best to stay inside.

Billy watches Hamish attempt to hold the plank level while hammering nails into the window frame. He's not sure why Hamish is doing this, but he offers to hold the wood steady while Hamish works.

When Billy gets home, his hands dirty and beginning to callous, his mother frowns.

"And he was boarding up the windows? But why?" she asks

"I don't know," says Billy with a shrug. He rubs his nose absentmindedly, and his mother's frown deepens as she, equally absentmindedly, wipes the smudge with a damp kitchen towel.

"I hope Hamish is doing ok," she says, half to herself. "Ever since Emmeline passed..."

Billy swats his mother's hand away and shrugs again. "Whatever," he mumbles, pushing his way past her and into the living room. He nearly collides with his father, who laughs gently and steadies him by the shoulder.

"Watch where you're going, kiddo," Frank says. Billy nods reluctantly. Frank watches him plop down on the couch and shakes his head, but the quirk of a smile still plays on his lips. He turns to his wife and gathers her in his arms, planting a kiss on her cheek. "Have you seen what Hamish has been up to?"

Mary leans into his embrace and breathes in the scent of soap and woodfire that seems to exist permanently on his skin. "Yes, Billy was just saying that he's boarding up the house. Do you know why?"

Frank shakes his head. "No, no clue. Maybe a storm is coming?"

Both of them peer upward out of the window, looking for signs of an ill wind as if the mention of a storm will suddenly darken the sky, as if the mere word could call fat droplets of water down to the earth.

From this angle, they can just see Hamish's house, a tall square of pale pink against the clear blue sky. Not a storm cloud in sight.

Hamish himself is but a speck, surveying the house and observing his handiwork. He walks up to one of the windows and knocks on the plank of wood. Satisfied, he makes his way back inside.

"Well, if there's to be a storm," says Frank, holding his wife closer to him, "Hamish is the only one who knows about it."

Chapter 2

When the storm hits, it is a fire inside of Hamish's heart, a red-raw pulse that spreads from his chest and down to his toes. He thinks he screams, but he's not sure if the scream is ripped from his lungs or if it's happening inside of his head.

There is a crunch.

At first, he thinks it's because he's knocked over his glass of whiskey and the crystal has shattered.

But then he wonders if it's him that's crunching, bones and teeth gnashing against some secret inside of him. There is a mischief in his blood, an echoing giggle that sharpens his teeth and pulls on his limbs like he's nothing but a child's toy.

He is coming apart at the seams, stuffing

spilling onto the rug.

Hours or minutes later—he's not sure anymore—he finds himself on the floor. There is lead in his lungs and he gasps for breath. His body is not his own, or at least, it's not the body he has known for forty years. He flexes his hand and his nails, now long and sharp, carve four shaky lines into the wood floor. He looks at them as if they are a foreign language and if he stares hard enough, he just might be able to translate them.

He turns his head to the side and finds himself framed in the shaft of moonlight that triggered his transformation. There is a calmness inside of his head, and he knows this is it for now, for this full moon at least. He is still more man than beast for this one, his wolf-form a wisp at the back of his head, a mere mention in his muscles.

He is still on the floor, and when he attempts to push himself up, he finds that he cannot move.

So, he closes his eyes and focuses on breathing. At some point, he lets sleep, or something very like it, take him away.

He dreams that Emmeline is there, her

hand a soothing cold on his forehead. She presses her lips to his temple and whispers something in his ear. She smells like wisteria.

Consciousness takes the dream away, and he blinks against the brightness of the sun. There is a roaring in his head, but it soon fades enough for him to realize that there is a knocking on the door.

He lifts his head, but his arms don't follow. He stays pinned to the floor, his body still not quite his own.

A lunar-hangover.

The knocking persists, and he thinks, at some point, he is able to call out to the visitor. At the very least, he hears a snap, and the chain barring the door thunks to the ground. The door creaks open.

There's a whisper of "Oh, Hamish."

Then, sleep truly takes him.

————— ◆ —————

Mary Appleton gently closes the door to Hamish's bedroom. Frank stands in the hallway. Their frowns are reflections of each other.

"How is he doing?" asks Frank.

Mary sighs. "As well as can be expected. He's still sleeping, but his body..." She pauses, thinking again of the misshapen limbs, the russet fur lining Hamish's face so different from the gray-tinged scruff of his beard.

"It was the man who stayed above the pub last month, wasn't it? Tim said..." His voice trails off as he shakes his head.

Mary knows what he is hesitant to say: Tim had lost three cows that week, and he told them it was an animal that did it. "*A large wolf, almost as big as the cow, but definitely stronger anyhow,*" he had said. "*Large teeth. The cows were ripped apart. It's that Newcomer, I know it is.*"

Mary suppresses a shudder. "Right, well. Hamish wouldn't do that. He's our friend and we have to help him."

Frank smiles fondly at his wife. He knows that look: there will be no changing her mind now. Besides, she's *right*. He has known Hamish almost his entire life, much like everyone else in Mims. He is a neighbor and, even with a second form, he always will be. "We'll do whatever we can," says Frank.

Chapter 3

"This is highly irregular," says Arthur. "As the Mayor of Mims, I—"

"Oh, sit down Arthur," says Frank.

Arthur does as he's told but not without a few huffs of indignation. Almost everyone in Mims is gathered at the Wizard & Goose, and they look at Mary Appleton expectantly. The sun slants through the window, illuminated dust particles dancing above everyone's heads. The smell of beer and freshly baked bread lingers in the air. The pub looks smaller in the daytime, with its dark wood paneling and vibrant red booths that look too bright with sober eyes.

Mary clears her throat. "Thank you for coming here today," she begins. "I would like to discuss Hamish Kelly. It would seem that the bandage on his hand was in fact from our Newcomer last month. Last night's full moon has hit him quite hard."

"I knew it!" shouts Tim from the back of the room. His short laugh is accompanied by a slight whistle as his breath passes through the gap between his front teeth. He takes a gulp of lager to reward himself for his astute observations.

"Yes, Tim," says Mary patiently. "You did. And now Hamish is affected. His body tried to transform last night, only it wasn't complete, and he isn't well."

"Why should we help him?" asks Rose, the owner of the pub. "If he ends up anything like the Newcomer, he could wipe out our livestock. Or worse."

"And what do you propose we do instead?" asks Father O'Brien.

The room is silent as they all consider the alternative that is too terrible to say out loud. A hunting rifle hangs above the bar in the back of the room, and a few people look at it briefly before averting their eyes with a grimace.

"Well, that's settled, then," says Frank. "We're helping him."

"Yes," continues Mary. "Now, Hamish will be unable to cook for a few days, so I think we should get a roster going, so we can get his meals covered. Then, we should consider the very real possibility that the next full moon will mean a more...complete transformation. We should build a safe environment for him to do so. If he does end up as vicious and beastly as the Newcomer, we won't have a chance to find out. We'll keep him from hurting himself or anyone else."

"Has anyone talked to Ginny?" asks Rose.

As the local witch, Ginnifer Ips is perhaps the only citizen of Mims qualified to handle such matters. She is absent from the impromptu town meeting, but that is not unusual. She lives on the outskirts of town, in a small cottage hidden in the trees. Often, the only sign that anyone lives out there is the lavender smoke from her chimney, wafting upward, reaching for the clouds.

Father O'Brien speaks up first. "I saw her yesterday evening for our discussion on the afterlife. She said she would be foraging and may be in the woods for a week or so."

Mary nods. "We'll wait until she gets back then. And maybe she'll have something to help Hamish with the transition."

With their plan settled, the townspeople go their own ways. Some head home, to begin baking a casserole or sorting through their pantries for their best jar of jam. Father O'Brien even donates a bottle of 20-year bourbon that he keeps for special occasions. "For a bit of comfort," he says with red cheeks. Rose donates two loaves of bread and her Famous Meatloaf. Tim and Frank team up with Harold, who is not quite a carpenter but skilled in woodworking nonetheless, to start planning Hamish's transformation room.

"Now, it's not a cage," says Frank. "Remember that. It's got to be a little homey, at least. But practical. Strong walls. A good lock."

Harold nods. "Should be easy enough."

Chapter 4

Hamish grips the door frame.

They've built an artificial wall in the corner of their barn and the resulting room is not the largest, but it is not the smallest either. It's comfortable enough, even though it lacks any natural light. There is a cushion in the far corner, plush and lined with velvet.

Mary is fiddling with her necklace as she observes him. He is standing up—an improvement over last week and an accomplishment over the week before that. The only meal he's been able to keep down is Rose's Famous Meatloaf and the lack of nutrition is beginning to show. Mary has known Hamish almost her entire life, and she has never seen him look so frail, so broken.

She wonders if it is his natural age coming

through, something she shudders to think will happen to her soon. They are only two years apart after all.

But then she sees his hand gripping the door frame, and it's as if she can see the curse of the bite eating away at his body, his muscles and bones forever splintered between two truths.

Hamish is at a loss for words. He can't shake the feeling that he's been nothing but a lazy lout the past four weeks and this—this safe haven, built by his friends and neighbors and even Harold, who has held a grudge against Hamish for twenty years because he once beat him at a card game—is too much.

"Mary, I..."

"Oh, hush," she says. She can see the words he's searching for in his eyes. "Of course, we would do this for you. You're our friend, Hamish. And we love you."

"I know I haven't been...the most friendly. Since Emmeline passed."

Mary squeezes his shoulder. "Don't you worry about it. We all need space from time to time."

Hamish smiles, but the muscles in his face feel awkward and out of place. Although he cannot see it, he knows the moon is above them. There is a brief spark of fire in his veins. His wolf-form growls, deep and low in his belly. "I think you should leave me be, Mary."

"Yes, of course," she says. "If you need anything, we'll be close by."

"That's what I'm afraid of," he mumbles as she closes the door. The lock clicks into place with a dull thud.

The crunch is louder this time, like a twig snapping in the forest, a predator catching his scent. He would run if only his legs would move. He is on the floor, staring at the paisley rug they have given him. It's incongruous with the beastly pain in his body, and he laughs, thinking of how selflessly Mary Appleton has given up her favorite rug to help Hamish feel at home.

He could have loved Mary once—when they were young and too foolish to know what they needed. He remembers his hands on her waist at the school dance, her dark curls tickling his nose as she leaned close.

What was the song they danced to?

Something slow and sweet, like violins in the clouds.

The moon sings a similar song, painfully alive and twisting through his blood. He screams, but it is no longer a voice that leaves his mouth.

———◆———

The howl echoes across Mims.

The sound sends shivers down Mary's spine, but she keeps to her post outside of the door.

Frank comes running around the corner, having stepped away to check the outer wall of the room. "Are you ok?"

Mary nods. "It was just—" There is a loud thunk against the door. "Oh, Frank, what if the door doesn't—"

But before she can put words to her fear, the fear scratches at the door. The wood splinters.

Once. Twice. Then splits.

Mary steps backward just in time, as a large paw swipes at the air. Franks grips her arms and slowly pulls her back with him.

"Just, stay still," he whispers in her ear, and they do just that, breathing the same rhythm, in and out, with the pulse of their heartbeat rushing in their ears.

The wolf swipes at the door again, teeth ripping the wood as if it were paper. There is a deep growl coming from the wolf's belly, so low Mary isn't sure if it's real. The wolf steps forward through the wreckage of the door and turns.

She can see Hamish in the crystal blue of the wolf's eyes, and Mary smiles sadly because they look just like they did when Emmeline died, an ocean wave bereft and aimless. Hamish always did need a direction to head toward, something to do with his anxiety and dreams.

The wolf steps forward but pauses to sniff the air. Something on the wind, a light lavender breeze, grabs his attention. With a shake, he trots off in the direction of the woods.

Mary watches the wolf slope away. "Frank?" she whispers. "Did anyone ever warn Ginny about Hamish?"

Frank is silent, but the tightness of his grip is answer enough.

———•◆•———

The leaves crunch beneath Ginnifer Ips' boots, and she whistles along to the dying song of the trees.

There is a bottle of homemade wine in her basket and a few wild mushrooms she picked last week. She is headed toward the church, following the winding dirt path from her home to the center of town.

She is not particularly religious, preferring the sermon of worms and crows over the Word of God, but her conversations with Father O'Brien always lift her spirits, so she swings her basket in tune with her song and makes her way through the forest.

Soon, she notices another sound—an alternate footfall that is not her own. She pauses, taking a deep breath into her chest. She holds it for five seconds, listening to the forest, the home she knows almost as well as her own mind.

She is not alone.

She feels his presence deep down in her blood, and there is a sudden flash of the future in front of her: a vision of russet fur, a laugh, a kiss pressed to the back of a hand, and a purple flower by the window.

She looks to her right and opens her mouth to speak, but the words are snatched from her throat by the clasp of teeth on her neck. She grabs the beast and holds him tight as they tumble backward.

Chapter 5

It's Father O'Brien who finds her.

Ginny is lying in the leaves, her tangled hair forming a halo around her head. Her basket is next to her, mushrooms scattered about. The bottle of wine has somehow survived.

Curled against her and wrapped in her arms is Hamish, naked and bruised. It would be embarrassing—intimate even—if it weren't for the blood.

Father O'Brien calls out that he has found her and leans down to check her pulse, searching desperately for a flutter of life in her chest. But it's hard to see where the blood begins and where Ginny's throat ends.

He says a prayer while the search party gathers around, Frank and Mary at the forefront of the group. Harold removes his hat and holds it solemnly to his chest. Rose looks away, her mouth hardening into a frown. Tim, who was never one to let death get in the way of a raunchy quip, keeps his mouth shut and lowers his eyes to the ground.

"She's still alive," says Mary, kneeling down. "We need to get them inside."

Frank takes off his jacket to cover Hamish before he and Father O'Brien loop their hands under Hamish's shoulders, gently moving his body out of Ginny's embrace. Although she is slight and her hand is slender, it drops to the soil with a thud that reverberates like a clap of thunder.

There is a second of oppressive silence.

Mary can hear her heartbeat in her ears, and then all she can hear is the earth beneath her feet moving, dancing to the beat of an ancient drum that is surely only in her chest. Suddenly the trees that surround them are full of birds, squawking, hooting, and shrieking, competing with the sound of the wind as it picks up the leaves scattered on the forest floor.

There is a sense of something coming, a shift in air pressure. Whatever it is, it rushes toward them with the ferocity of hellhounds. The feeling circles them tighter and tighter until the ground begins to bubble, like water in a cauldron.

When the bubble bursts, it spews an army of ants, scouts that lead the way for a colony of iridescent beetles, gleaming gemstone-bright in the descending dark.

Then, the worms come.

Grayish and wriggling, they gather up Ginny's spilled blood, the bits of her that were ripped asunder by the wolf's bite. They diligently stitch her back together, blood and bone, flesh and soul. When the last worm falls back down into the soil, swollen with stolen blood, Ginnifer Ips is breathing the slow, steady rhythm of deep sleep.

———◆———

She sleeps for days. The only sign of her attack is the shiny pink scar that runs down the length of her neck and disappears into the collar of her nightgown. Her skin is neither too cold nor too hot.

She rests peacefully.

Hamish sits by her side, head bent in fear that he has passed his curse onto her. Mary told him how the worms had put her back together, and he hopes they took the wretched mischief that his bite would have given her.

Moons come and go, and still, Hamish sits while Ginny sleeps. She wakes up once, in the middle of the night, and Hamish grabs her hand to calm her down.

He doesn't let go.

Mary brings him tea and sits in the corner, knitting. The click of the needles is like a clock, ticking time forward, closer to the next full moon. Father O'Brien sits opposite Ginny and prays to his God and to hers.

When Hamish's body reaches its limit, he slumps back in the chair and closes his eyes, sinking into a fitful sleep.

———◆———

It is a week before the next full moon.

Hamish has relented and allowed Frank to set up a cot next to the bed so that he can sleep while staying close. His hand still strays to

Ginny's, as if she will float away and only he can anchor her to the ground. Father O'Brien is reading, though the gentle snores coming from his direction would say otherwise. Mary continues her knitting, almost done with a scarf for Billy.

A rustle of fabric, so loud in the heavy silence of waiting, causes Father O'Brien to look up. Mary stops her knitting.

Ginny shifts underneath the quilt and looks over at Hamish, her normally bright eyes foggy with sleep and confusion. But then the memory of russet fur, a bloody embrace, and leaves crunching beneath their bodies come back to her and she sighs, squeezing Hamish's hand.

She turns to Father O'Brien. "Liam," she says, "And Mary. I need your help."

She describes a book, an innocuous leather-bound tome worn with use. There is no title on the cover or spine, she warns. "But you'll know it when you see it. We'll need it before the full moon."

"Why?" asks Mary, but sleep has already taken Ginny again.

There is still smoke coming from the cottage in the forest. The flames in the fireplace are crackling gently, lit by an unearthly kindling.

Father O'Brien crosses himself, but Mary has a feeling that it is more out of habit than any particular comment on Ginny's proclivities.

The hut is dark and cozy, filled with the measured chaos of one who *collects*. Books spill out of the bookcases, herbs are drying from the rafters, and precious rocks line the windowsill.

There is a pale milky liquid bubbling in a glass beaker attached to an arrangement of copper tubes emptying into a cauldron, a low blue flame burning underneath it. The book next to it is slim, brown leather worn to a soft caramel, and open as if the architect of the contraption had stepped away only a moment ago.

Father O'Brien leans over the text and reads, mumbling under his breath. "It's Latin," he says. "The Song of the Worms."

"Do you think that's the book?" Mary picks it up and flips to the first page, angling it toward Father O'Brien so he can translate the title.

"The Worm Wood. The Book of the Worm Witch. One of the Nine." Below this, in hasty handwriting, are the words "If lost, please return to Ginnifer Ips, The Cottage in the Forest, Mims."

Mary flips through until she finds an illustration of a wolf howling at the moon. Father O'Brien translates again. "Temper a Lunar Transformation."

Mary nods and snaps the book shut. "That's the one."

———◆———

Temper a Lunar Transformation requires only a handful of ingredients, but the process is particular, with handwritten notations adding further specificity to each step. Mary follows along as best as she can, letting the rose and hibiscus petals stveep in warm water for the prescribed amount of time, stirring it with a silver spoon owned by her grandmother and only used on holidays. She waits by the pot, as it sits in the field, the stars above reflected in the liquid as if it is made of the night sky.

Hamish attempts to help, stirring the solution when Mary's eyes begin to close. She

TEMPER A LUNAR
TRANSFORMATION

Prepare   week   of   transition

MUST HARVEST RIGHT
BEFORE THEY WITHER

Steep hibiscus and rose petals in warm water
for three days; strain, set petals aside for later.

Grate   ginger   and   star   anise
and   stir   into   infused   water.
Let   settle   under   the   stars,   stirring
with   a   silver   spoon   every   few   hours.

3 HOURS

Once the first rays of morning sun touch the
edge of your cauldron, bring it back inside.

KEEP AWAY FROM SUNLIGHT!!!

BLUE
Fill a bottle with the hibiscus and rose
petals and add the infusion. Seal with
STRIP OF CLOTH, SENTIMENTAL
a cork wrapped with twine, chamomile
blossom, and a piece of willow bark.

ADD CREAM- MUCH BETTER!
Consume when the sun touches the horizon.

waves him off. "You should be resting."

Frank takes over, while Mary leads Hamish back upstairs and to his cot next to the bed he used to share with Emmeline. Ginny is lying in the middle, the quilt wrapped around her as if she has always been there. Hamish feels Emmeline's absence, but it does not hollow out his chest as it once did. The room is warmed by the hearts beating inside of it.

Ginny is awake and looking out of the window. Her eyes dart to Hamish when he sits down, the cot creaking beneath him. "I can feel it," she says. "The moon, moving, growing, like a child I'm going to give birth to."

Hamish blushes. "It's different for me. Like a song I can't get out of my head." Silence falls between them but it is too heavy for him to bear. "Ginny, I'm sorry about—"

"Did you see it too?" She's looking out of the window again. Her long hair is brushed to the side, revealing her scarred neck. He follows her gaze out of the window, but there is nothing there. Just the darkness of Mims. He asks what she means, but she is already sleeping again.

Chapter 6

When the full moon reaches its chorus, Hamish howls.

His thoughts are clear, just as clear as the liquid he had swallowed from the blue bottle sealed with chamomile and willow bark and a strip of fabric ripped from a forgotten blanket. He shakes off the pain easily.

Beside him, Ginny does the same, the gentle swish of her fur joining in with the cicadas' song and the low inquisitive hoot of an owl above. There is a white strip on her neck, a stark reminder of the curse-scar she now bears.

But she bears it well, letting the mischief settle into her bones and muscles, and she clenches her paws to feel the grass beneath her.

Hamish watches her in the moonlight, and he is struck with a memory of her walking through the forest, a moon ago, her boots splashed with mud and her long skirt torn.

There had been a sudden flash behind his eyes, a bright light that brought a vision of a purple flower and an amber full moon. He had felt the sunshine on his upturned face and Ginny's sun-warmed cheek as he pressed his lips to her skin that smelled like jasmine.

Ginny bumps her head against Hamish's, and he understands that she has the same memory. The same flash in the night had stung her eyes, woken up something inside of her even before the mischief-laced bite tore into her neck.

A sudden snap of a twig sounds in the night and with a joyous yelp, Ginny bounces off in the direction of the noise, intent upon a rabbit that she cannot see but knows is there.

Hamish follows, rounding the side of the house and brushing against the tangled remnants of the wisteria vine. It catches on his fur, but he pays it no mind, intent on the hunt before him.

The woody vines of the wisteria shiver slightly in the moonlight. It's been bare for almost two years, but it can feel the soil glowing beneath, turning with something new, something green.

It sits and waits for the sun to rise and its purple blooms to unfold.

Part 2

In the Field, Under the Moonlight

Chapter 7

Sorry.

She hates the word, yet Hamish keeps saying it. She grits her teeth against the sarcasm building in her throat, and she exhales the unspoken words while she closes her eyes, letting the morning sun warm her limbs instead of her frustration.

The coldness of the night did not bother her wolf, but now that the full moon has passed and the day has dawned anew, her skin prickles with goosebumps. It always takes her some seconds to feel human again, to coordinate her too-long limbs, to make her lips curve in a smile instead of baring her teeth in a snarl.

Hamish must feel the same way, she thinks. He is always quiet in the morning, his movements slow and deliberate. He avoids eye contact, and she follows his lead, though she is always aware of him and the space he takes up.

They dress themselves using the spare clothes from one of the packs they have hidden around the woods, in fallen trees, or hanging high from a tree branch. She can see him out of the corner of her eye, and she can hear the soft grunt as his knees protest. She has already pulled a loose cotton dress over her body, and she ties her hair back with a ribbon before they begin their walk out of the woods.

He bumps into her as they amble across the field. His skin is warm, the fabric of his cotton shirt rough against her arm. "Sorry," he mumbles, deliberately slowing his step so that he is behind her.

Hamish is always sorry.

This is her third transition and Hamish's sixth. Although each has been easier than the last, their routine is still uneasy. Hamish is both too courteous and too cautious around her, which, in turn, makes her feel awkward and quiet. He treats her like a glass sculpture, and she is starting to believe him.

It makes slipping back into her human form all that more difficult.

They walk back to Hamish's house, the sound of cicadas taking the weight out of the silence between them. The dry grass tickles her ankles, and her bare feet are caked in mud.

She wouldn't have it any other way though: the pulse of the sun overhead, the coolness of the soil underfoot. She is, first and foremost, a witch, and her blood is tied to the earth.

Hamish's home is a pink Folk Victorian house that sits in the middle of the field. The remnants of a farm are scattered around it like a sentimental skirt that is kept despite the ragged hem. In the distance, sits the Appleton farm, segmented by wooden fences. The morning is hazy, but the brightness of the red barn in the distance cuts through the fog.

Ginny looks up at Hamish's house, her gaze landing on the upstairs bedroom window where she spent a month recovering from her wolf bite. She thinks of Hamish as he bent over her, hands clasped in silent prayer. She was sleeping for most of it, drifting among stars and infinite truths while her body healed, but she does remember the constant presence of him.

He smelled of smoke and pennyroyal.

They climb the porch steps and, in silent agreement, sit in the matching rocking chairs, two dancers who know their choreography well. There is a fresh bowl of water and two dish towels on the low table between them. Hamish dips a cloth into the water and rings it out, before handing it to Ginny. It rained the previous night, making the fields muddier than usual.

They may become beasts every full moon but that's no reason to forgo manners altogether.

She washes her feet and her hands, then she presses the cloth against the back of her neck. She thinks of it as stretching the wolf away, though more and more, she's noticing some wolf traits hanging around longer, providing her with an acute sense of smell or much keener eyesight.

Out of the corner of her eye, she sees Hamish doing the same, wiping his fingers and then his palms. There is a faint tan line on his finger where his wedding ring usually sits. He never wears his ring during a transition.

As they enter the house, the screen door creaks, announcing their arrival.

Mary calls out from the kitchen. "Breakfast is on the table."

Although Mary is the same age as Ginny and only two years younger than Hamish, there is something soothingly maternal about her. She has indeed taken it upon herself to act as their caregiver and to welcome them back to their humanity with fresh crumpets and hot coffee.

Hamish presses a hand to his stomach, feeling the familiar hollowness that comes after a full moon. He has never caught an animal while in his wolf-form and has never felt the craving for raw flesh while running through the open fields with Ginny by his side. He has thought about it—how good a fresh deer must taste to his wolf tongue—but then he remembers the feeling of his teeth ripping into Ginny's neck, giving her this curse she did not ask for and certainly did not deserve, and he finds himself holding back in the chase, his paws just slightly sluggish as they push against the soil, never really using his full strength.

Mary hands him a coffee mug and kisses his cheek in welcome. "Good morning, Hamish. How was your night?"

"It was alright," he says, settling down at the kitchen table. Although there is a formal dining room through the door to his right, it hasn't been used since his wife, Emmeline, passed away a few years ago. Besides, the kitchen is more welcoming, with its bright yellow walls and lace curtains, the warmth from the oven chasing away the night.

Ginny slides into the chair across from him. She's learned that she rarely feels hungry after her transition, but she hasn't the heart to tell Mary this. She sips her coffee and breaks apart her crumpet, pushing food around on her plate like a sullen child until it feels appropriate to excuse herself.

Hamish raises a hand in goodbye, while Mary draws Ginny into a hug with promises that she will see her later.

When the door swings shut behind Ginny, Mary frowns and looks at Hamish with her hands on her hips. "You should at least escort her back home."

Hamish grimaces. "It's a curse, not a date. Besides, I don't think she needs the man who ruined her life acting as a chaperone. She's an adult."

Mary gives him a sad smile and grips his shoulder. "You didn't ruin her life...I'm sure she doesn't feel that way."

Hamish shakes his head and slides his chair back from the table with a grunt. "I'm going to get some rest," he mumbles.

Upstairs, the mattress creaks as he sits. He should shower and change his clothes before getting under the covers. Emmeline would have a fit if she saw him right now, his hair tangled and his clothes wrinkled.

There is still dirt caked under his fingernails, and he hasn't shaved in a few days, the grey scruff of his beard making him look older than his forty years. He feels older too, though his wolf feels young. Sometimes, in the dark, by himself, he admits that he misses the wolf. He envies its youth.

Then, he reminds himself that he *is* the wolf. It is not some separate entity using his blood and bones.

His hand hovers over the wedding ring on his nightstand. He always removes it before a transition. Once, he couldn't imagine ever taking it off—was sure that he would feel naked without its weight. Emmeline used to take her wedding ring off before gardening and would inevitably forget to put it back on. It often lived in a trinket dish by the kitchen door. Now, it lives in a jewelry box in the closet. He wonders if it's time to do the same with his. At the very least, he decides to leave it on the nightstand for now.

He settles back into the bed, his thoughts about Emmeline melding with Ginny.

Although they are two very different women, who hold very different spaces in his life, he can imagine them as friends, two fiery souls bonding over some fault or other of Hamish's.

He's sure he has plenty for them to choose from.

Then, like clockwork, he remembers the vision he had three months ago, the vision that circles in his mind, a song he cannot forget. He sees a dancing purple flower against an amber full moon. He feels sunshine on his upturned face and Ginny's sun-warmed cheek as he presses his lips to her skin that smells like jasmine.

Will those moments ever become reality? He lets the question hang in the air. He's not sure he'll ever be able to answer it.

As he pulls the quilt tighter around himself, he thinks about last night. He can remember the transitions well enough, though the colors of the world are all gloomy golds and blueish grays. When he closes his eyes, he recalls the silhouette of trees, the call of an owl, the smell of damp. The last thing he thinks of before sleep takes him is how Ginny's eyes glowed in the starlight.

———— ◆ ————

Ginny smells the lavender smoke before she sees it and, as she rounds the corner, her little cottage in the woods comes into view. The smoke curls high above the trees, an offering to the clouds.

Inside, the air is stilted, too warm. She opens the window and settles down on the small bed beneath it, filling her lungs with the Spring morning, all dew and orange blossoms.

Her hut is small and made smaller by the things she has collected over the years. Towering stacks of books, magic or otherwise, line the perimeter. The counter in the small kitchen is littered with herbs and scribbled notes and spell-making contraptions. The hearth, forever smoldering with a low purple flame, is home to a cauldron, though she is not currently using it.

She sighs, half comforted by her familiar surroundings and half frustrated by a growing feeling of worry that has been gnawing on the edges of her thoughts. In the solitude of her home, she takes a deep breath and lets the worry wash over her.

She looks around the cramped, dusty room and wonders if she could ever share this with Hamish. She tries to imagine him sitting at her table, but the image blurs, too far-fetched to ever solidify.

She thinks about his gentleness, his patient smiles, and how effortlessly he seems to handle the wolf inside of him.

Then she thinks about his politeness, so thick it has since turned into a wall between them. As wolves, they understand each other. Their connection is immediate, unspoken. They move like extensions of each other. But as a human, he feels so far away from her.

Does he regret biting her? Most likely, but the scar that runs down her neck and over her collarbone binds them to each other whether he likes it or not. There was never a conversation about whether they should spend their transitions together; they did and they would continue to do so. But that was as far as their relationship went.

More likely, he would rather have been bound to Mary, whose presence always makes him smile. When he looks at Ginny, he grimaces.

She may be in tune with nature now, but she wasn't always. She has had her rebellious years, the years of taking what wasn't hers to take, spilling blood and lies as easily as she breathes.

She has come a long way since those days, but still, they are a part of her. She thinks about sharing that with Hamish—sharing the entirety of her with him—but she can only imagine Hamish's grimace twisting further, her indiscretions turning him into a gargoyle of scorn and cold concrete.

The secluded nature of her cottage used to be comforting, a sweater to shield her from the elements, yet as she sits by the window, tapping an unsung song on the sill, loneliness blooms in her chest.

Chapter 8

The full moon hides behind the clouds, but Ginny can still feel it. Hamish can too and he throws his head back to sing a song to the celestial bodies above.

The howl is heard across Mims but no longer induces a fearful shiver. Some chuckle to themselves, thinking of Hamish Kelly and Ginnifer Ips, surely the oddest couple that Fate could have thrown together. Others ignore it entirely, the sound as normal as a freight train passing by every four weeks on its way to some unknown destination.

Ginny feels a growl growing, but it is not in defense or a warning. Her tail flicks back and forth, and she leans downward. She wants to run and Hamish obliges, echoing her stance until she bounds to the left with a yelp. He follows, reveling in the stretch of muscles, fur slicked back from the wind. He slides to a stop in the middle of the forest, his predator eyes searching for Ginny.

There is a rustle to the east, and he turns just as a deer wanders into the clearing.

Then, there, to his right is Ginny, stalking closer to the deer, so low to the ground her belly will be covered with dirt in the morning. He has no urge to go after the deer, but he can feel the excitement vibrating in Ginny, so he stands still as she creeps forward.

When she pounces, it is with teeth bared and jaw snapping. There is a tussle of fur and hooves. The deer bucks, his antlers pushing Ginny backward. There is a yelp, and then suddenly the deer is running away. Hamish barks once and starts to follow, the excitement of a chase thrumming low in his haunches.

It takes him a second to realize that Ginny is not following, and when he turns around, she is on the ground. He can smell her blood, coppery and floral, and his hackles rise out of instinct.

The deer's antlers have sliced a tendon in Ginny's back leg, and it is bent under her at an awkward angle. She lets out a soft whine.

He will need arms and legs to carry her back to safety. It is still a few hours from sunrise, and Hamish is beholden to his wolf until then. So, he settles in close to her, sharing his warmth, and rests his head on her back, waiting patiently until the moon has started her descent back into oblivion.

———— • ◆ • ————

The wound wasn't so bad in the moonlight, but the morning sun slants down on it, highlighting the jagged angry lines in her pale skin. The blood has barely stopped flowing, and Ginny grits her teeth as she tries to sit up.

Hamish has wrapped her in one of his flannel shirts, and she buttons it with shaky movements until he gently takes over, his fingers making swift work of the task.

When he finishes, he looks at the sweat on her brow and her clenched teeth, and something seems to shift beneath them like the earth has begun to quake. But the earth is still; it is his own body that has shifted, as he bumps his head against hers, a gesture he has only done in wolf-form. He holds her for a second before saying, quietly, "I'm so sorry I have given you this curse."

She raises her hand to his cheek, his stubble sending sparks against her skin still so sensitive after the transition. He leans into her touch. His smoke and pennyroyal scent fills her entire world. She bites her lip, wishing she was brave enough to kiss him. "It's not a curse, Hamish."

He grunts, indicating that he doesn't quite agree. "Let's get you home," he says.

———◆———

Mary is no stranger to blood—she does have an unruly son, after all—but the cut on Ginny's leg is deeper than it initially looked, with angry, red edges that look ready to soak up an infection in a heartbeat. The bleeding has slowed since Hamish carried Ginny over the threshold and gently laid her down on the couch.

But it is still coming, and Ginny looks paler by the second.

Mary presses a towel to the wound and looks up at Hamish. "Maybe we should call

Dr. Randall?"

He thinks of the doctor who must be close to eighty years old by now. The last time he went in for a physical, Dr. Randall, who delivered Hamish as a baby, called him Henry and misplaced the stethoscope twice.

"I can do it," he says, picking up the needle and thread.

Ginny is on the couch, awake but her eyes are heavy-lidded with exhaustion. "It'll be ok, Mary," she says through gritted teeth. "I trust Hamish."

Mary frowns but she shifts out of the way, letting Hamish takes her place.

His hand is warm against Ginny's thigh and she leans back, letting her head rest on the arm of the couch. The window is open, and Ginny watches the lace curtains dance in the breeze. It's a cloudy morning, the air heavy with the threat of rain.

When the needle bites into her skin, she makes a hissing noise. Mary holds her hand as Hamish works, and she distracts herself by counting the things in the room.

One couch, sagging but comfortable, encased in a soft blue fabric that hugs her like the sky.

One reading chair, stiff but reliable, sitting by the window with thin curtains, mended twice with fading yellow thread.

Two pictures on the wall, one of Hamish and Emmeline on their wedding day and one of Hamish when he was in school, his lopsided grin and ruffled hair hinting at a mischievous soul, ready to cause trouble. She bets Hamish was always up to something when he was younger, ready in a blink of an eye to seek an unknown adventure.

Ginny is half asleep by the time he's done and silently, Hamish gathers her in his arms.

"She'll have to stay here for a while, I think," says Mary as they make their way up the stairs.

"Whatever she needs..." he says quietly.

Although there is a spare bedroom, Hamish decides to give her the primary bedroom. There is an en suite and the bed is larger. Besides, she is already familiar with it.

Mary watches Hamish as he gently lowers Ginny to the bed. Watches as he pulls the quilt up and over her shoulders, wrapping her up like some kind of ephemeral thing that could slip from his grasp any minute now.

Ginny stirs and whispers something—

his name, Mary thinks—and Hamish nods, agreeing to her request.

The bed bounces slightly under his weight as he sits down beside her. He remains sitting, straight-backed, but lets his head rest against the headboard, his arms folded sternly across his chest.

He is asleep before Mary even closes the door.

Chapter 9

Ginny spends the next two days in bed. Rain has come and gone, leaving a fresh green smell in the air. The window, always open, brings tidings of wisteria blooms.

Mary returned home the day before, with the reminder that she is only a phone call away. Hamish and Ginny are in the bedroom, eating stew that Hamish made last month and defrosted. It's good—a hearty and warm broth with a delicate balance of spices and a hint of sweetness.

Kind of like Hamish, she thinks with a smirk.

After dinner, he checks her sutures, careful not to touch her leg any more than necessary. His politeness is busy rebuilding the space between them, and she yearns for the connection that she had barely had a chance to grasp.

She had hoped that they were beyond this when he nuzzled into her touch the other morning and she told him that his bite was not a curse. *He* was not a curse.

Covered in dirt, with her leg bleeding and burning with pain, she felt, briefly, the connection she feels when they are wolves, the wholeness that comes from being so close to him.

Perhaps she is foolish to expect more from him. He still loves his late wife Emmeline; does he even have room in his heart for Ginny? Not that the two cannot exist at the same time. Hamish can still honor his commitment to Emmeline while letting the wall between him and Ginny fall. She just doesn't know how to show him that it's possible.

He asks her if there is anything she needs before sleep and she yearns to say that she needs *him*: needs his arms around her, needs the weight of his hand on her hip, needs the scratch of his stubble against the back of her neck as they drift off to sleep, framed in the pale moonlight slanting through the window next to the bed.

Instead, she says, "No, I'm ok, Hamish. Thank you."

———— ◆ ————

The rain has come again, lashing angrily against the window, reluctantly closed. The room is damp and Ginny settles deeper under the covers.

Her leg is healing, but still sore. The sutures will need to come out soon, and, in the meantime, they become itchy. She distracts herself by sneaking glances at Hamish as he reads his newspaper. He shaved yesterday, and he looks younger.

The storm rages on.

"Hamish?" She motions to a book on the nightstand. "Will you read to me?"

He looks startled but recovers quickly, swapping out his newspaper for the cloth-bound green book. He begins to read, his voice melding with the thunder. "'You will rejoice to hear that no disaster has accompanied the commencement of an enterprise which you have regarded with such evil forebodings...'"

She pulls the blankets closer around her, though Hamish's voice is all the warmth she needs right now. She will have very little reason to stay in this room after today but she is not ready to admit this.

Not yet.

So, she soaks up this moment, however small, and carves out a little hole in her heart where she can keep the memory safe.

———— ◆ ————

Frank grabs two beers from the cooler. He hands one to Hamish and they cheers, the brown glass clinking a sharp contrast to the soothing sounds of the evening. The storm has cleared, leaving purple clouds vibrating against the bruised yellow of the sunset.

The sun inches closer to the horizon and the cicadas pick up their tune. Behind them, the sound of Mary cooking dinner trickles out of the open window. The air turns, crackling with coolness, and Hamish and Frank sit on the porch, watching the sheep in the distance.

A few yards away from them, Ginny is lying on a quilt spread out in the grass, her hair golden in the fading light. Her leg is healing well, but she still keeps it stretched out at an awkward angle. Her arms are extended outward, so her hands rest palm-down against the earth. "To help me heal," she had said.

"I reckon it'll be a mild Summer if you wanted to get your field ready for some peas. Maybe some cabbage," says Frank.

Hamish nods. "Yeah. I was thinking of getting some tomatoes for this year."

"Onions would be good," says Frank. He sips his beer. "Tim says he won't replant his this year, so you could get some good money at the Sunday market."

"What about strawberries?" calls out Ginny.

"We'll do strawberries," says Hamish, struck, not for the first time this week, by his use of the word *we*.

What began as an absentminded, convenient thing has become a selfish wish, pinging against his sternum. He has no right to hold onto Ginny as if she belongs here, in this home, but he finds himself doing just that. Despite his guilt, he must admit that Ginny has settled into her wolf-form quite well. He can see a kinship between the two halves, both wild things who don't mind bowing to the stars and the earth.

Of course, he has a feeling that if Ginny changed her mind, the stars and earth would have no say in the matter.

He hides his thoughts in his bottle of beer, which he finishes in one quick motion. "Another one?" he asks Frank.

"What about me?" asks Ginny with a crooked smile.

He nods and when he hands her the bottle, she angles her hand so that it closes over his. She pauses, her palm cool from the rain-soaked soil. "Sit with me?" she asks.

When Mary comes out to tell them dinner is ready, she hesitates to disrupt the scene. Ginny is leaning against Hamish's side while she drinks her beer (not that she should be drinking alcohol while she is still recovering from an injury, thinks Mary). Hamish has his arm around her shoulders, and they are watching the sunset while chatting with Frank about how best to divide and prepare the field for seeds.

Strawberries and onions! Mary is delighted at the thought of seeing the Kelly farm green and lush again.

"We could even get the orange grove fixed up again," Frank is saying.

"That would be lovely," says Ginny.

Hamish nods. "The trees aren't too bad off. It might take a full season to get a decent yield though." He uses his beer bottle to point to a lone tree around the side of the house. "The peach tree has fared better than the rest. We'd have better luck starting with that one."

"The wisteria is already coming back," says Ginny.

Hamish pauses, as if he hadn't realized that the woody vines have started sprouting again. "Indeed it is," he says with a soft smile.

Chapter 10

The cottage is the same as it was the last time Mary was here, slightly crooked with weather-beaten wooden slats.

There is something alive about the structure, the way it slants to the side as if watching her as she watches it. Perhaps it's the fact that the chimney is always filled with lightly-scented smoke. Even though Mary knows no one is home, she still knocks gently on the door before entering.

Last night, while cleaning up at dinner, Ginny had taken Mary aside and asked her to stop by her hut. "I'll only be here for another day or so, but there's a salve...it'll help with the scar," she had said. "I also wouldn't mind a fresh pair of clothes," she added, looking down at Hamish's robe.

Mary understood and nodded. Besides, in that second, she had a spark of an idea, a half-formed thought that grew overnight and propelled her to rise earlier than the sun to fetch Ginny's requested items.

She finds the salve quickly enough. It is labeled and right where Ginny said it would be. Then, she folds a sage green dress and slips it into her bag. She adds a pair of slippers and, on a whim, grabs a pair of pearl earrings and a gold hair comb. Then, she turns about the room looking for the real reason she agreed to come here.

Mary finds it in the same place she found it last time, the brown leather-bound book resting on the counter, open to a random page. Father O'Brien has been helping her practice Latin, and as she flips through the pages, she searches for a particular word.

When she finds it, she copies the text onto a scrap of paper, making mental notes about what ingredients she has in her pantry and which ones she will have to purchase from the corner store on the way home.

———◆———

Frank finds her in the kitchen, her cheeks flushed from leaning over the simmering concoction on the stove. "Whatcha cookin', love?" he asks, kissing her cheek.

"Oh, just...a little something for Hamish."

If he was any other man, he would be jealous of Hamish Kelly and the amount of space he takes up in his wife's thoughts.

But he has never felt threatened by Hamish.

He knows Mary and Hamish had once flirted with a romantic relationship, but it never went anywhere. Although he and Hamish grew up together, they have never been close, always friends of friends, one step away from each other in social circles—though that has changed in recent months, with Frank finding a sort of burgeoning camaraderie with Hamish.

And anyway, he does not begrudge Mary her history, just as she would never punish him for something he did before their relationship. But her hesitation is suspicious. She's hiding something.

"What are you up to?" he asks, cautiously.

"I just thought...you know how slow Hamish can be to share his feelings. And

Ginny, well, she's clearly lonely but too uncertain of Hamish's feelings to say anything..."

Frank raises his eyebrow, waiting for her to continue.

"I just thought, maybe I could give them a little push in the right direction."

He shakes his head. "Don't go messing around with things you don't fully understand, Mary. It won't end well."

"I know what I'm doing," she insists, looking at the dark simmering liquid in the pot on the stove. She gives it a clockwise stir, once, then counter-clockwise, halfway, to agitate the herbs soaking at the bottom.

He sighs, "Well, I want no part of it."

"I'm not asking you to be a part of it."

He makes a sound of disbelief in the back of his throat. He will get pulled into it; he always does. Yet, as always, whatever annoyance he feels is short-lived. He pulls her close, his hand on her waist. "Just be careful."

"I always am," she insists, her voice sharp, but then he kisses her until she laughs against his lips, and she returns the kiss in kind, only vaguely aware of a disgusted "Yuck" coming from Billy as he passes through the kitchen. When Frank pulls back, she puts both of her hands on his chest and says, "Go on now, I've got work to do."

He laughs, pressing one last kiss to her cheek. When the kitchen door swings shut behind him, Mary returns to stirring her potion, smiling at the memory of Frank's hands on her hips.

Chapter 11

If Hamish had known that dinner would be candle-lit and punctuated with wine, he would have worn something other than a faded flannel shirt and jeans.

At the very least, he would have shaved again.

Mary has outdone herself, he thinks, looking at the table she and Frank have set up outside. They might as well be at that fancy new restaurant the next town over—the little Italian place with the marble tables and cloth napkins.

Ginny is wearing a sage green dress, the neckline cut a little lower than she normally wears. Along with a salve for her leg, Mary brought back a few of her personal items, including the dress and a pair of dangly pearls earrings.

In the fading daylight with her hair pinned up, the scar on her neck is visible but it doesn't make Hamish grimace as much as usual. He has gotten quite used to it while Ginny has been staying with him. Her leg is almost completely healed, and when she walks, there is barely a limp to suggest the injury even exists. She will be returning to her cottage in the woods tomorrow, so Mary suggested they have dinner before she goes.

At least he remembered to bring a gift for the Appletons, a bottle of homemade wine which Mary pours into mismatched glassware. Frank proposes a toast to "friends and community and a bountiful Spring."

But they no sooner sip to Frank's toast when Frank slides his chair back. "Should go check the grill. See how dinner is getting along," he says quickly.

"Oh, and I'll go fetch us some more bread," says Mary hastily, snatching the suspiciously still-full basket from the table.

Hamish watches his neighbors scurry back into their house. He turns to Ginny to see if she knows what that was all about, but there is a playful smirk on her face that stops his words in his throat.

She is holding in a laugh, he can see it in the line of her shoulders, and her cheeks are flushed with the cool Spring evening.

He can always feel the moon above him, tied to him, his eternal mistress. But at this moment, the ties snap, reeling back to hit him with the realization that the moon's control is a fickle thing compared to the woman sitting next to him. She is his moon, with pale skin and stars in her eyes, full lips smiling down at him, a Cheshire moon of rosy pink.

Her words from the other morning have been echoing in his head, *It's not a curse.* But he can't shake the feeling that he has shackled this young beautiful woman to a grouchy, lazy lout of a man, and he wishes he had bitten anyone but her.

When he opens his mouth, he hears himself saying as much, his words bitter and cold. "I wish it had been anyone other than you." The realization of what he has said washes over him, his cheeks turning warm. He can't remember the last time he blushed. "Sorry, I'm not sure why I said that."

Sorry.

That dreaded word.

She ignores it in favor of a smirk. "It's probably the love potion that Mary spiked our wine with. Or at least, that's what she was trying to do." She sniffs her glass, her eyes closed as she shifts through the scents. They are sharp in her nose. "I think what she actually did was make an infusion to turn the tongue bitter."

She dips her finger into the glass and brings it to her lips, sampling a drop of the wine on her tongue. "It's quite weak, though." She chances a look at Hamish. He looks like he is going to be sick. His regret is palpable, stinging nettles on his tongue. "We just have to sit in silence until it wears off," she says graciously.

The sound of a record player wafts through an open window in the house. Mary and Frank are nowhere to be seen, but Ginny would bet that wherever they are, Mary is hoping that she and Hamish are falling madly in love. It's an easy thing to do—mistake the Latin word for love with the word for bitter, after all.

Hamish can feel the potion sliding down his sternum, harsh like moonshine. He moves his tongue around the bitterness, searching for words that can be stretched beyond the lines the potion has drawn in his mind. "What if I don't want to sit here in silence?" he says gruffly.

She arches an eyebrow. "What do you propose we do instead?"

He gives her a gentle, yet wolfish smile. Perhaps he too has noticed the wolf inside slipping through the cracks. He stands up and offers her his hand. She purses her lips, curious, and allows him to pull her up from the chair. This close, she can see the moon in his eyes, can feel the pull in his pulse. His heartbeat is identical to hers as he holds her close against his chest, the buttons of his shirt pressing into her belly.

Few in Mims know that Hamish can dance. Mary, of course, would know. They went to a school dance once, many moons ago.

Yet, Ginny had not known that Hamish was so quick on his feet, at least when he has two feet. They have run beside each other as wolves, leaping and chasing, but this is new.

His hand is on her lower back. She feels the stubble on his face as he leans closer.

Smoke and pennyroyal envelop her, and she takes a deep breath, letting him shuffle her away from the table, hips swaying in time to the beat, finding their rhythm just like the pianist feeling their way over the keys.

They sink into the moment. The breeze carries the smell of the wisteria vine alongside Hamish's house, and Hamish closes his eyes, his head resting atop Ginny's. When the song ends and shifts into another, Ginny leans back to look at Hamish. She can feel the bitterness fading and thinks it must be the same for Hamish because his eyes wrinkle with a soft smile.

As if in compensation for the overwhelming bitterness, her tongue turns sweet and the words tumble out of her mouth like strawberries and orange blossoms.

"I know you can't see it yet," she says, "but your bite was not a curse, and I will never feel that way about it. I think..." She pauses, biting her lip. "I think, I would very much like to stay for a bit. Here, with you."

He makes a hoarse grunt in the back of his throat, unlocking the words he has kept caged for too long. "I want you to stay. Here, with me."

She leans into him again, her head against his shoulder and they sink back into their dance, drenched in moonlight.

Epilogue

A Picnic At Mims Cemetery

Ginnifer Ips does not talk about her death often, but there are some things that Moira needs to know.

They walk, hand-in-hand, through the forest. The air is hot, sticky-sweet like the maple syrup Moira likes to drown her pancakes in. Her mother's hand is cool, her palm a soft refuge.

They pass Ginnifer's old home, her cottage hiding among the trees. She is not sad to see the chimney cold, the tops of the trees no longer obscured by pale purple smoke that has traveled through the brick column for the past twenty years. She loved that cottage, crowded with remnants of her craft and her life, curated by the mischief in her heart.

But she loves her home with Hamish more.

At first, the space scared her. She has spent a lifetime and more in carefully contained spaces. The fields were vast, the house large and made even more spacious with open windows and country breezes that smelled of grass and flowers. The world pulsed around her, empty but with a potential she wasn't sure she could tame.

Yet Hamish, with his soft smile and patient hands, turned the soil and fed the earth. She'll never forget the breathlessness of seeing that first hint of green. She saw it grow from root to bud to petal to fruit.

The space didn't scare her so much after that.

They continue down the dirt path, trees towering over them in silent contemplation. The forest begins to thin. They can now see the bell tower of the church framed against the pale morning sky.

"Are we there yet?" asks Moira. She is seven and would rather be at home, reading a book or climbing a tree, or helping her father feed the chickens.

"We are," says Ginny, as dirt becomes cobblestone.

The entryway to the Mims Cemetery is

in front of them. The gates are open. The stone archway is carved with oak trees whose limbs form into stars. Ginny knows it was a decorative choice, but she has always seen the oaks as gods, ever watchful over their charges on earth—a thought she has done well to keep herself.

She does not begrudge the religious nature of the cemetery, just as she would never belittle any who believe such things (and Mims is chockfull of Believers, she knows).

Yet, some things are better kept silent, lest they cause unnecessary rifts.

The cemetery is quiet, save for the song of cicadas and the doves cooing overhead. They pass through rows of grave markers, smooth from age but well-tended nonetheless. She wonders if she will see Father O'Brien this morning, pulling weeds or cleaning the marble slabs as he does most mornings.

She gives Moira's hand a soft squeeze. "Here we are."

They kneel by a headstone, the stone slab that denotes her final resting place. The stone is covered in moss (she has explicitly asked Father O'Brien not to worry about tending to her headstone. She's perfectly capable of doing it herself, thank you). The inscription is still legible:

GINNIFER LOUISE IPS

1909-1922

A few feet away, lies Emmeline Kelly. Her gravestone is spotless, a soft milky marble with wisteria flowers carved into the edges. She remembers visiting with Hamish the first time, a few months after they danced in the moonlight, and she told him she didn't want to leave. He showed her Emmeline's grave and together they left a bouquet of purple flowers.

Later, she dreamed of Emmeline and her bright smile and gold curly hair. In the dream—if it was a dream—they sat underneath the wisteria vine on the side of the house and Emmeline held the bouquet they had left at her grave. They dug their toes into the earth and laughed about Hamish's forgetfulness, such as his habit to leave his watch by the bathroom sink even though he has knocked it into the water while shaving several times.

They held hands and watched the sunset

and Emmeline told Ginny to take care of Hamish. Not that he needed it of course. Hamish has always been too independent, too ready to care for others before himself.

If anything, Ginny promised to let him care for her. "It gives him focus," Emmeline said, biting into a strawberry. "He needs something to love, or the restlessness will eat away at his heart until there's nothing left."

Ginny has packed a picnic for today and will leave a small bowl of strawberries and a purple flower on Emmeline's grave before they leave.

"There's nothing buried here though," says Moira, her hand pressed against the earth.

Ginnifer smiles. "Well, there wouldn't be, would there? I'm right here."

She gives Moira a poke in her side. Moira giggles. "So why are we here, Mommy?"

"I need to tell you about your family." She sits her basket down and spreads a quilt over the grass, settling down in the center. She pats the space next to her and Moira joins her, crossing her legs. "You see, I wasn't born a witch. I was made."

"Like how Daddy made you a werewolf?"

"Kind of. That's a different sort of mischief." A mischief that she didn't ask for but couldn't live without, she thinks, remembering one of her earlier transitions and how Hamish had rested his forehead against hers, apologizing for a curse he had not meant to pass on, but one that she already loved, one that fit in some sliver of a hole inside of her heart that she hadn't realized was there. "It's not a curse," she had told him and she says the same to Moira now. "Remember that. You may take after me now, but this mischief may yet take hold of you, and if it does, it will be right."

Moira shakes her head. "I don't think it will. It's not meant for me. I think it's meant for my brother."

Ginnifer frowns. "What do you mean?"

Moira shrugs and is quickly distracted by an ant climbing a long blade of grass. Ginny presses a hand to her belly. She had only suspected but wasn't sure.

Moira takes after her more than she had realized.

"Let me braid your hair," she says. Moira dutifully turns and sits, straight-backed. "I need you to listen to this story while I do so.

Can you do that?"

Moira nods. Storytime is revered in the Kelly household, after all.

"Once, a long time ago, I was just a little girl, not too much older than you. I wasn't special, but I was born into a special family. A family of witches and warlocks and even sorcerers who could cheat death. But I wasn't one of them. My parents were beside themselves in grief. How could they birth a such a beautiful baby girl, with no mischief in her blood? No secrets hiding in her fingertips?"

Moira turns and very solemnly places a hand on her mother's arm. "You're special to me, Mommy."

Ginnifer smiles, her heart so full it makes her chest hurt. The sun is just overhead, stretching around them like saltwater taffy. She continues braiding her daughter's hair, picking a daisy or two and a few honeysuckles to weave in between her ruby gold locks. "Well, my parents could not accept me as I was and were going to give me up for adoption. But then Mr. Thomas arrived. He stood on the doorstep and told them he needed an... assistant. A protege. He did not care if his assistant had any particular peculiarities or affinities. He asked for me."

She remembers the shadow Mr. Thomas cast, as dark and cool as the gravestones around her now. She hid behind her mother's skirts, peeking around the rough gray fabric to watch this stranger shake hands with her father. He didn't mind that her hair was tangled or that she had blackberry stains on her lips. He smiled at her and placed a too-warm hand on top of her head.

"She's perfect," he told her mother. "Such life in her eyes."

"She's not...a witch," her father had said hesitantly

"I can make her one," said Mr. Thomas.

"My parents had heard of such spells," says Ginny. "But you need an energy source that is not for the faint of heart. My parents wouldn't sully their hands to do it, but this stranger, with his money and shiny shoes and his gold tooth...well, he could take the black spot on his soul. All they needed was to sign a three-year contract, handing over guardianship of me. At the end of the contract, he would return me, in one piece, and I would be a witch."

"Were you scared?" Although the sun is still above them, Moira feels like it has turned cold, her mother's words resting on her shoulders like snowflakes.

"Not at first. But then my lessons began."

Ginny pauses. She has told this story once before, to Hamish the night before they said their wedding vows. She left a fair bit of it out, and she'll do the same now, even more so considering Moira's age.

This is what she leaves out:

The long, tortuous hours in the dark.

The tiny cuts Mr. Thomas wore into her skin. "To soak in the magic," he would say, his gold tooth sparking like fire.

Mr. Thomas's breath on the back of her neck and the callouses on his hands as he reached for her in the dark.

The peculiar pressure of soil on her chest, suffocating but comforting all the same.

The sounds the worms whispered in her ear as they wriggled against her, upset that their home had been invaded.

Her scream, soil spilling into her mouth...

...her throat...

...her lungs...

"The lessons were not kind," she says. "They hurt and they changed me. And then they broke me. And life left my chest. The spell had failed."

"Then what happened, Mommy?"

"The worms tasted my pain in my tears, and they decided to help me. They told me the secrets of the earth, secrets that not many know. They showed me magic and as they knit me back together, they gave me what I should have been born with."

"Is that why the worms in the garden always come up when you walk by?"

Ginny laughs, her voice as light as the leaves rustling in the gentle breeze. "Yes, they're checking up on me. I am the first in their line. They called me Little Wyrm, after their ancient god that no one else remembers."

She doesn't speak her other name, the one she gave herself so many moons ago, long before she met Hamish, the name that she no longer uses but is just as proud of.

The Worm Witch.

Magic given can just as easily be taken away. She has always been grateful for her gift, even as it tore her apart. Although the worms were once her wardens, they have become her friends.

Moira is quiet for a few seconds, thinking about worms and her mother—the ethereal being who can cure sadness with a kiss and whose hands hold her steady when the wind blows too strongly. "What happened to Mr. Thomas?"

Ginny peers up at the tree above them. A crow sits on the branch. It stops its preening to look at her, cocking its head to the side. It caws a soft warning and then goes back to its morning activities.

She thinks of the months she spent in darkness. They had already set her grave marker on the ground and it stood proudly against the winter sky as she clawed her way out of the soil.

Mr. Thomas was furious. His blood had run through her veins and some of it stayed—the worms could not clear it all out—so when the sun shone down on her once again, she felt the fire of his rage in her chest. She swallowed it down, brushing it off as if she had merely eaten something that had disagreed with her.

She hasn't felt it since, but she knows he

is still out there, his footsteps reverberating against the earth with each step, knows he still takes air into his lungs, knows his heart still beats an evil rhythm.

She has never lied to Moira before, but now she must. The lie tastes of burning salt. "He's gone. He died a long time ago."

Perhaps Mr. Thomas will come for her yet. She trusts in her power and in Hamish's, too. They will handle the storm when the clouds break.

Moira fingers the end of her braid with a small smile, but she is still uncertain of this story and why it is important.

As if reading her thoughts, Ginnifer says, "I need you to understand that there are people out there who will try to take what has been given to you, Moira. Only, it is not theirs to take."

"The worms can take it though..."

"Yes, it was once theirs. They are free to take it at will. But as long as you honor their power and you treat the world with kindness, they will be your allies. You are second in their line, Moira, and they will welcome you just as they have welcomed me. Do you understand?"

She nods.

Ginnifer takes Moira's hands in her own and gives them a squeeze. "Ok, now what should we have for our offering?"

"Mmm..." Moira's lips pucker to the side in an exaggerated thoughtful expression. Her eyes light up, golden cinnamon in the late morning sun. "An orange!"

Ginny takes two oranges out of their basket and hands one to Moira. Diligently, they work on peeling the fruit. The red flesh inside looks pink through the pith. They separate their oranges, and Ginny hands one of her segments to Moira, as Moira hands one to her mother.

It's a symbolic gesture—sharing your sustenance with your loved one—and Moira knows the practice well.

When she bites into the orange segment, juice runs down her chin, making her giggle. The sun joins their picnic, breaking over the tops of the trees as morning turns to afternoon. They nibble on crackers and olives, slices of peaches with clotted cream, and roasted almonds smothered in honey (Billy Appleton has recently gotten into beekeeping).

Moira tells Ginny a story about the owl who is roosting in the Appleton's barn and together they come up with names for owlets that will hatch in a few days. When their bellies are full and Emmeline's gifts have been left, they pack up their picnic. Before they go, Ginny places a hand on her grave marker, the stone warm against her palm.

Moira is gripping her other hand, squeezing it with impatience. "Mommy, can we feed the chickens when we get home?"

Ginny tears her attention away from her grave. "Yes! Of course!" she says excitedly. "But first we need to run some errands." Moira's shoulders slump. Ginny laughs. "It'll be fun."

"Promise?"

"Always."

They leave the cemetery, and Ginny leaves her thoughts of Mr. Thomas there, with her gravestone covered in moss. She focuses on their errands: on remembering to buy more coffee and flour, on making sure they stop by the library to pick out a new book for Moira's bedtime. She wonders if she has time to take Hamish's watch to the jeweler for repair.

But, mostly, she focuses on Moira, and

she smiles because she loves the way her daughter skips along beside her, the way she rambles on about the things they see as they walk, the way she giggles so readily at a truly terrible joke.

She loves that Moira grips her hand like she is about to float away and only her mother can keep her tethered to this world she has only just met but loves just the same.

She doesn't even mind that Moira's hand is sticky with orange juice.

fin.

ABOUT THE AUTHOR

J. LYNN CARR may be a newly published author, but she has been writing for many years; it just took her a very long time to finish something. Before writing, her main creative outlet was painting, and she still considers it a significant part of her life.

Carr resides in Austin, TX, with her husband and their two beloved dogs, Milly and Freddie.

www.ingramcontent.com/pod-product-compliance
Lightning Source LLC
Chambersburg PA
CBHW031547310726
48971CB00008B/2664